The Yuckee Prince

LARRY O'LOUGHLIN

BLACKWATER PRESS

For Monica C2 P3
Georgina

© Copyright Larry O'Loughlin
First published in 1995 by Blackwater Press,
Hibernian Industrial Estate, Greenhills Road, Tallaght, Dublin 24.
Produced in Ireland by Folens Publishers.

Editor: Deirdre Whelan
Cover Design/Illustration: Steve Simpson
ISBN: 0 86121 805 1

British library cataloguing in publication data.
A catalogue record of this book is available from the British Library.
O'Loughlin, Larry: The Yuckee Prince

Contents

Chapter 1

This is a story about:
> A Prince,
> A Witch,
> and
> A Cat.

Well, no. That's not quite right. This is my story. I'm telling it, and I'm a witch. So, I suppose what I should really say is, this is a story about:
> A Witch,
> A Prince,
> and
> A Cat.

But before you run off screaming:

"Mammy! There's a wicked, horrid witch telling me a story."

Let me put you right on a couple of things.

Firstly, I'm not a bit horrid. In fact, I'm really rather nice, and not at all bad-looking – even if I do say so myself.

And secondly, I'm not the slightest bit wicked; most witches aren't.

Oh, I know you've heard about the one who put Sleeping Beauty to sleep for a hundred years, and the other one who kept Rapunzel prisoner in the tower. But that doesn't prove anything, does it?

I mean, how many witches do you think there are in the world?

Hundreds?

Thousands?

Millions?

Gazillions?

You don't know?

Well I have to be honest, neither do I, but I'd guess that it's somewhere between thousands and millions.

And that's my point.

If there are that many witches in the world, and you've only heard of a few bad ones, then most witches must be good, mustn't they?

And I'm one of the good ones.

Now, let me ask you another question.

How many bad princes have you heard of?

None?

I thought not, and neither had I, not until the day I came face to face with Prince Alysious Tripod Jefficus, the Yuckee Prince.

Most princes I'd heard of were the brave, handsome, dashing type. You know the sort, always rushing off to slay dragons or rescue princesses in distress and that sort of thing.

But, if there are as many princes as there are witches (and I suppose there must be at least that many) then it stands to reason that if there are a few bad witches, there must also be a few bad princes.

Mind you, I wouldn't mind betting there weren't many who were as bad as the Yuckee Prince.

To look at him, with his big blue eyes, his dimply cheeks and his long golden curls you'd have thought he was a perfect little angel.

And so he was, when things were going his way or he wanted something.

"Mammy," he'd say with his sweetest smile.

"Can I have another lollipop?"
or
"Daddy, may I have another slice of cake? "
or
"Mammy, may I stay up another hour or so?"

And if the answer was " Yes " then everything would remain perfectly peaceful and happy. If, however, the Queen or King replied, as most parents would,

"Now dear, you know that too many lollies are bad for your teeth."
or
"No dear, I think another piece of cake would make you feel ill."
or
"No dear, you know that you'll be too tired in the morning."

Then the sweet little angel would turn into a raging, screaming demon.

He'd throw himself on the floor, kicking and punching, and holding his breath until he turned blue in the face. Then he'd jump up, run across the room,

grab the cat and jam him into the goldfish bowl.

Next, he'd tug and pull at the curtains until they came tumbling down into one big heap. And when he'd finished with the curtains, he'd start throwing and breaking anything he could lay his hands on.

Oh, he was a real little cutie all right, and God help anyone who tried to stop him when he was in that sort of temper, because he'd kick and scratch, and bite and spit, and pull hair and be just about as nasty and horrid as anyone could be. In fact, he was absolutely yuckee!

The poor King and Queen! They just couldn't control him at all, and neither could anyone else. That was why no one who knew anything about him would ever go near the palace, and why every day there'd be a long line of butlers, cooks, maids, gardeners and the like rushing to leave.

They'd go running down the road, clutching their bags and belongings while he stood on the balcony throwing stones, pulling faces and calling them names.

It was the only kingdom in the world where every night you'd find the King and Queen up to their elbows in washing-up, or sweeping their own rooms and making their own beds.

They really were a pitiful pair.

So, you can imagine how delighted they were when one morning a letter arrived inviting them to the birthday party of Princess Tara, a princess in the nearby kingdom of Urse.

"Oh, how delightful," smiled the Queen.

"How delightful. Just think how pleasant it will be to be treated like a real king and queen for a change. Not having to do the washing-up, or the cooking or the sweeping, but having it all done for us. It will be wonderful. Quite, quite wonderful," she giggled in delight, as she passed the invitation to the King.

"We must get ready to leave at once. I'll take my blue dress, and my green dress, and my yellow dress. I'll take my black shoes and my red shoes and... "

As the Queen chatted on, the King read the invitation quietly, then he made one of those loud "Ahem" noises that you may have heard your own parents making when things weren't quite as they should be.

"There may be a slight problem here, my dear," he said softly.

"Did you read *all* of the letter?" and before she could answer he continued, "I mean this handwritten note on the bottom from Sir Damus, the Chief Herald of Urse."

The Queen shook her head slowly.

"I thought not," said the King, sighing. "It says, 'Perhaps the young Prince should stay at home, as I am sure he will find the journey most tiring.' "

"Oh," said the Queen.

"Oh, indeed," said the King.

And then for some time neither of them said

another word. There wasn't anything to say, because they both knew that what Sir Damus was really saying was,

"On no account bring that little horrid brat of yours with you."

And they couldn't really blame him.

The Yuckee Prince had been horrid to him on their last visit to Urse. Once, while Damus was asleep the Prince had covered his beard with raspberry jam. Another time he'd filled Damus's bed with thorns and nettles and waited outside to hear him scream. And if that wasn't bad enough, he'd even painted the old knight's donkey with green, white and yellow stripes.

No! They were in no doubt. The note meant that if they were going to go, then they would have to go alone.

"Oh dear," said the Queen, with a long deep sigh. "It would have been so nice, so very, very nice."

As they sat there sighing and feeling sorry for themselves the cook, the two hundredth and twenty first that year, stormed in, picked up the invitation and in very large letters wrote:

"I Quit"

Then he stormed out leaving the door open behind him.

Soon, the whole palace was alive with the sound of screaming, yelling and crashing dishes, as the rest of the staff went racing for the gates with the Yuckee Prince rushing behind them throwing cups and plates and screeching,

"Go on, ya bunch of sissies run... and good riddance... good riddance to ya all... "

The King looked across at the Queen. Almost pleading, he asked,

"Do you think we could find anyone who would take him off our hands for a few days? Just a few little days?"

"I doubt it," said the Queen. "Unless... unless we gave an extremely large babysitting fee, but even then I doubt it."

"Oh, if only we could find someone," sighed the King, "because I really would love to go."

"Go where?" yelled the Yuckee Prince, rushing into the room "Where are we going... where are we going?"

"We... er... er... er... " stammered the King.

The Prince looked down and saw the invitation. He broke into a big smile which grew wider and sweeter as he read it. Then, suddenly the smile disappeared and his face went red with anger. He rolled the invitation into a tight little ball and hurled it across the room.

"How dare he!" he fumed. "How dare that great fat, ugly old man suggest that I shouldn't go!"

And he jumped onto the table and began stamping his feet in anger.

"Now, now," said the Queen meekly. "It is a long way, and you know how easily you get tired."

"Don't, don't, don't," screamed the Prince, running up and down the table kicking the plates, cups, knives and forks across the room.

"I don't get tired. I don't. I don't. I don't... And anyway, if I can't go you can't go... I won't let you. So there!"

"Not even for one hundred of those special, giant lollies they make in Urse?" said the King. "You know, the ones as big as your arms?"

"No!" snapped the Yuckee Prince angrily.

"How about one hundred and fifty?" offered the King.

"No!" screamed the Yuckee Prince.

"Two hundred?"

"No!" shouted the Yuckee Prince.

"Two hundred and fifty?"

"No!" said the Yuckee Prince, but not quite as angrily this time.

"Three hundred?"

"No!"

And on and on they bargained until it was finally agreed; the Yuckee Prince would stay behind if they would bring him seven hundered and thirty of the giant lollipops (those of you who know these things will realise that, that's two lollies for every day of the year).

"But who will mind him?" sighed the Queen.

"Oh, don't worry about that. I'm so lovable that people will be fighting to mind me," smiled the Yuckee Prince with his sweetest smile. "After all, they're just plain, ordinary people, but me... well, I'm a real little prince."

"You're most definitely a real little something," the King muttered under his breath. "Most definitely."

Chapter 2

The next morning the King and Queen were up bright and early, and feeling so cheery that they were humming and whistling as they made their breakfasts and did the washing-up.

By the time they came to load their bags onto the royal carriage they were so happy at the thought of their little holiday that they were actually singing and skipping.

"A real king and queen again, a real king and queen again," the Queen sung to herself, as she danced around the carriage. "A real king and queen again."

The Yuckee Prince didn't join in the singing and dancing but he did feel quite pleased with himself. Wouldn't you, with the thought of those seven hundred and thirty giant lollies? But it wasn't just the lollies!

Now, it could be that they'd forgotten, or it could be that they just decided there was no point in asking him to make a promise they knew he wouldn't keep, but the King and Queen hadn't once asked him to promise to be good while they were away. So, as far as he was concerned, that meant he was free to do just whatever he pleased... and he really liked that idea.

In fact, it pleased him so much that he hadn't done one naughty thing all morning. Well, he had tied the dog to the cat's tail, but that didn't really count because he hadn't been caught.

"Well then," smiled the King, when he'd loaded the last big trunk.

"That's everything loaded. Let's head off into town. We can drop the little Prince off and be on the road to Urse within the hour."

He leaped up into the driver's seat and tugged on the horses' reins. The horses trotted briskly forward. "I'm sure the reward will encourage someone to take him," he whispered to himself. "It has to!"

What a shock he had waiting for him!

Maybe everything they heard over the next few hours was true, or maybe it was just that no one was too overjoyed at the thought of having the Yuckee Prince as a house guest – you'll have to make up your own mind on that.

Out of the three hundred and sixty houses they tried, everybody said they'd be only too pleased to have the Prince stay with them; indeed, they'd be overjoyed, thrilled to bits, absolutely delighted... etc... etc... etc.

Sixty-eight had everyone in the house down with measles.

Seventy-seven had chickenpox.

Eighty-eight had whooping cough.

Ninety-nine had flu.

Fourteen were leaving to stay with relatives in other towns.

Twelve were expecting relatives from another town to stay with them.

And two didn't even bother to answer the door, although the King was sure he could hear someone whispering,

"Sssssh!"

and

"Are they gone yet?"

The poor King and Queen. They'd started their journey smiling and singing, but now after a whole day of driving around and knocking on doors they felt like crying. No one would take the Yuckee Prince, not even for two days.

As they turned their coach around to make the journey home, they felt sad and tired. Even the Yuckee Prince was tired. In fact, he was so tired he didn't scream or shout once. It was all he could do to pull the stuffing out of the seats of the coach.

"Ah well," sighed the King. "That's it. We've tried every house in town. No one can take him. So, I guess we just can't go. Ah, what a shame!"

"It would have been so nice," said the Queen sadly. "So very, very nice. Still, we've tried everyone."

But of course, they hadn't tried everyone. And there was one person who had absolutely no idea just how yuckee the Yuckee Prince could be.

How could she? She had only been living in the kingdom for a couple of days.

Just as the King gave a second sigh, thinking

20

about how nice it would have been to put his feet up for a couple of days, a light came on in the little cottage at the edge of the woods.

"Do you think there's the slightest chance?" he began hopefully.

"Well, it's worth a try," the Queen interrupted, knowing what he was going to say next.

"After all, she is a newcomer and she is certain to want to impress us."

Then in a low whisper, so the Yuckee Prince couldn't hear, she added, "And after all, she hasn't been here long enough to know what he's really like."

Suddenly they were whistling and humming again as they turned their coach towards the little cottage.

Chapter 3

I don't suppose I have to tell you who that one person who'd never heard of the Yuckee Prince was, do I?

I do?

Well, dear me. I'd have thought you would have been able to guess by now. Anyway, it was me – Witch Way. I was the only person in the whole kingdom who'd never heard about the Prince.

Now, when I say I'd never heard of him I don't really mean that I'd never heard of him, exactly. I mean, I knew there was a Prince called Alysious Tripod Jefficus. I also knew the name of the King and Queen, and the butcher and the baker and the candlestick seller, and all their families. We witches like to know these things when we're going to a new kingdom...

No. When I say I hadn't heard of the Yuckee Prince, I mean I hadn't heard just how horrid and yuckee, he was. Like you, I thought all princes were good and noble and kind and... boy, was I wrong.

"Well, if you didn't know how yuckee he was, how do you know all the things you've just told us?"

I hear you ask.

And a very good question it is too, if you don't mind me saying so. The answer is quite simple. I found out later.

If I had known what he was like you can bet your little brother (or sister) that I'd have suddenly come down with something nasty, horrible and catching, too. But I didn't know.

So, there I was fresh out of the Grizelda Grimwood Academy for Wizards and Witches, with my Diploma in Witchcrafts hung proudly on the wall, all my books, potions and lotions in their proper place, and my feet up on the table enjoying a nice cup of

nettle and twig soup (I'll send you the recipe if you want).

Tiddles, my cat, was stretched out in front of the fire enjoying his second favourite hobby of sleeping. Eating sausages was his first favourite hobby. Suddenly–

Tap... Tap... Tap

There was a soft tapping on the door, and a tired voice was calling.

"Witch Way. Oh, Witch Way. Might we talk to you a moment?"

I looked at Tiddles with surprise. I wasn't expecting anybody, and as far as I knew he wasn't either.

"I wonder who that can be?" I said, taking my feet down and putting my soup cup up. "I'm not supposed to start working here for another few days." I walked over and opened the door. When I saw the King and Queen, well I got such a surprise that you could have knocked me off my broom with a budgie's feather, as we witches say.

I still had enough sense to make a little bow, the way Dame Grimwood had taught us and mumble,

"Your Majesties, please do me the honour of stepping into my humble home."

They shot a quick glance at each other, and I think I saw the Queen cross her fingers for luck, then the King smiled wearily.

"Firstly, Witch Way let me say how welcome you are to our Kingdom. I'm sure you'll bring great honour to your school, yourself and the kingdom while you are with us," he winked at the Queen, who seemed to be crossing her eyes as well as her fingers.

"Please don't think us impolite if we don't come in on this occasion. It is just that we are in an awful hurry to get to the Kingdom of Urse... er... something came up unexpectedly."

"We have to be there as soon as possible," added the Queen, who I think, although I can't be sure, was now crossing her arms and legs as well.

"The thing is," said the King, "the journey would be much too tiring for the Prince, who as you can see is already very tired."

I looked at the Yuckee Prince who was almost more asleep than awake and nodded.

"And, well because this was sort of unexpected and what with the palace staff leav... er... on leave, and everyone in town either sick or going away or expecting visitors, we were sort of wondering, " said the King, almost in one breath, "would you be able to look after him for us? It would only be until the day after tomorrow... "

"Really, only a couple of days," said the Queen, almost pleading.

"And we really would be most, most, most, most grateful."

Well, double-knock me off my broomstick with a budgie's feather!

There I was, only three days out of the Academy and two days into my first job and the King and Queen were already asking me for a favour. Wouldn't that make Dame Grimwood proud of me!

"Why certainly your majesties, I'd be only too pleased and... "

I didn't even have time to finish the sentence before the Yuckee Prince was pushed into my cottage. The King and Queen were rushing down the path as fast as their legs could carry them.

"Remember, only two days and seven hundred and thirty lollies," the King shouted over his shoulder. Then they jumped into the coach and shot down the road like a rabbit chased by a dog. As I closed the door I thought I could hear them yelling,

"We did it... we did it. We got rid of him. Two whole days without him. WHOOPEE! WHOOPEE!"

Now, I know that that should have told me something about the Prince but I was just too excited to think about it. I was so happy, I could have hugged myself.

Just think of it! Me, Wendy Way, only a witch for five days and already given the honour of looking after a prince. Hazel, my best friend at the Academy, would be green with envy when she found out. I'd probably get my name in *Witches' Weekly* and read out in the Academy. If I did a really good job, I might even get my photo hung in the "Famous Pupils" corner. It was so exciting!

I looked at the Yuckee Prince. Even half-asleep he looked just like one of those little angels that you see on Christmas cards. I put my arm around him and brought him over to the fire.

"Tiddles," I said, "this is the little Prince and he'll be staying with us for a couple of days."

Tiddles looked up, yawned and went back to sleep.

I turned to the Prince and gave him my best smile,

"And I'm Witch Way, little Prince. For the next two days we'll have great fun together."

"Ugh," he grunted.

He was so tired that he didn't even notice when he trod on Tiddles' paws – one at a time.

I led him into the visitor's bedroom. He kicked off his shoes, flopped down onto the bed, and was asleep almost as soon as his head hit the pillow. I tiptoed out of the room and went back to my chair beside the fire.

"Well, Tiddles we must be on our best behaviour for the next few days, mustn't we?"

Tiddles was too busy rolling around on his back trying to lick his paws better to even try to reply.

"Oh, don't be such a baby, Tiddles. It was an accident. Go into the kitchen and see if you can find another sausage to take your mind off it. I have to write and tell the Dame my good news."

While Tiddles hobbled off in search of food, I sat down and wrote Dame Grimwood a long, long letter telling her all about the great honour I'd been given. Then, just to round it off, I signed it,

From a very, very lucky
Witch Way.

Some luck!

Chapter 4

It was like Christmas Eve or the night before my birthday. There were butterflies in my tummy. My face was smiling by itself. Songs kept popping from my mouth, and hundreds and hundreds of happy pictures went spinning around and around in my head. It didn't matter what I tried. I was just too excited to sleep.

I read *The Foster Witch's Handbook* and *The Witches' Guide To Babysitting* from cover to cover. I took notes about things they said happen (such as children having tantrums or not eating when they're lonely). I copied the lists of "Things To Do" and "Things Not To Do" when babysitting. I counted sheep, broomsticks, buckets, witches, rabbits, puppies, kittens, goats, cows... the hairs on my head, and I even tried counting the freckles on my friend Hazel's nose (from memory, of course) but what was I doing when the sun came up?

Correct!

I was lying there wide awake.

"This is ridiculous," I sighed, turning over for the one gazillionth time. "I'll make one more try to get to sleep and if that doesn't work, I'll just get up." I closed my eyes, pulled the blankets up under my chin and...

"AAAAARRRGGGGHHH!"

The scream shook me out of bed.

"Wha... wha... wha... " I stammered, trying to push myself up from the floor. "Wha... wha... wha... "

"AAAAARRRGGGGHHH!"

It came again, shaking the whole cottage and sending Tiddles hiding under the bed in fright.

"AAAAARRRGGGGHHH!"

I couldn't think what it was or where it was coming from, then the hairs on my neck stood on end and my heart started beating like a drum. It was the Prince! The Prince was in trouble!

"Oh dear, the Dame will kill me."

I rushed into the kitchen, grabbed the poker, and charged into his room screaming a scream that would have scared a ghost and...

"About time, too," grumbled the Yuckee Prince, beating his hands on the bed. "I want my breakfast and I want it NOW!"

"But what about the wild animal or the... er... er er... er?"

"What animals, you silly, great goat? I want my breakfast NOW! NOW!"

He screamed again.

"NOW!"

Phew! He was all right! I wasn't in trouble! I was so delighted that he wasn't being eaten by wild animals or murdered by robbers that he could have brought the whole cottage tumbling down and I wouldn't have cared.

"Certainly, little Prince," I smiled with relief. "And while I'm doing that I'll leave Tiddles here to play with you."

I dropped Tiddles on the bottom of the bed, closed the door and walked back into the kitchen.

If the Prince wanted his breakfast then that's just what he was going to get, and it would be the best breakfast anyone ever had.

I pointed at the table, whispered the magic words and hey presto! There it was, a breakfast fit for a prince.

There was porridge, bacon, sausage, egg, mushrooms, fried potatoes, scones, cream, jam, orange juice, apple juice, milk and a big bowl of fruit. Just thinking about it makes me hungry.

I put it on a tray and pushed the bedroom door open ready to say, "Good morning, little Prince."

Tiddles was clinging to the curtains, screeching and trying to crawl away while the Prince stood there swinging a pillow at him.

"Oh good," I smiled, putting the breakfast tray on the bed.

"Pillow fights. I used to love that when I was younger. Now, eat up little Prince, then we can start having fun."

The Yuckee Prince threw the pillow on the floor and stared at the tray.

"Look at that," I whispered to Tiddles as I lifted him down from the curtains.

"He's delighted to see so much food."

As soon as his paws touched the ground, Tiddles shot out of the bedroom as if a pack of dogs were chasing him, and dived under the nearest chair.

"I'll leave you to enjoy it, little Prince," I said and turned to go, but as I did I noticed that one of my laces was untied and bent down to tie it – a good thing too! At that very moment... Whoosh!

A plate of porridge went hurtling over my head and smashed against the wall.

"Call this breakfast?" he screamed.

"Call this muck breakfast?"

And suddenly he was hurling cups, plates and saucers everywhere.

I jumped back into the kitchen as two sausages whizzed past my ear and landed besides Tiddles.

"I want a proper breakfast," he screamed, "a proper breakfast, and if you don't give it to me I'll tell the King and Queen that you were horrid to me, and they'll have your ugly, skinny head cut off, no mistake about it."

"Bu... bu... but little Prince, what's the matter with... ?"

"A proper breakfast," he screamed again. "A real, proper breakfast."

"But little Prin– "

"A proper breakfast. Not this muck. A proper breakfast."

Well, I knew what this was. This is one of those temper tantrums I'd been reading about in my books. He was only acting like that because he was feeling very sad and lonely, and if I did the right thing, the book said I could soon bring him back to his normal self. (Well, okay, so this was his normal self – but I didn't know that did I?)

But what was the right thing?

I didn't really know, but I supposed I couldn't go far wrong by letting him have what he normally had.

So, I tapped gently on the bedroom door and called, "And what would you like for breakfast, little Prince?"

"Jelly, ice-cream, custard, cream cakes, fizzy pop, trifle – all the normal stuff," he shouted. "And remember, if I don't get it... your head'll be off in a flash."

Jelly and ice-cream for breakfast! It didn't sound very "normal" to me, but then I'd never met a prince before. Maybe that was the sort of thing they always had for breakfast. I wouldn't have liked it, but still, if it made him happy!

I pointed at the table, said the magic words, and hey presto! The table was covered with everything he'd asked for: jellies, ice-cream, fizzy pops, cream cakes, everything. And I must admit, it did look rather wonderful.

"You can come out now, little Prince," I called, "everything's ready."

He came charging out of his room, red with anger, but as soon as he saw the feast on the table, he began clapping his hands, laughing and jumping up and down.

"Oh, you *are* wonderful," he cried, "you are the kindest, sweetest babysitter anyone could ever have. This is just what I wanted. The very thing." He scooped up two large handfuls of jelly and ice-cream and shovelled them into his mouth.

"Ang ow dig ya doog it so fasg?" he asked through the mouthful of food. "Ow?"

"What's that? How did I do it so fast? Well it's

easy for us witches, little Prince. We just... "

Suddenly, he was coughing and spluttering blobs of jelly and bits of ice-cream all over the table.

"You're a witch?" he said with shock. "A real witch?"

"Why yes, little Prince, don't you remember last night... "

"A real witch? With spells and potions to turn people into lizards and bats and all sorts of horrible things like that?" he carried on shaking with fright.

"Well, yes, sort of but... "

"The sort of witch who could turn a fellow into a frog or rat or toad, all because he was missing his mum and dad and got a bit upset and made a bit of a mess of his room and that?" he babbled, all in one breath.

"Well, I could but... "

"You wouldn't do it to me though, would you?" he pleaded.

"Of course not, little Prince," I laughed. "I wouldn't do a thing like that."

"Are you sure?" he asked, looking quite pale.

"Absolutely."

"Honest?"

"Honest."

"Witches' honour?"

"Witches' honour, I promise."

"Oh, OK then," he sighed, looking happier.

"I suppose that's OK."

And he started stuffing handfuls of cake and custard into his mouth all over again. Then he stopped.

"Do a spell for me."

"But I can't do... "

"Go on, just a bit of a spell. Make a rat or a giant or a dragon or something appear. Go on."

"But I can't just... "

"Go on," he said firmly. "Just one little spell, go on."

"But little Prince... "

"Oh, go on, go on, go on," he insisted, beginning to scream, half excitedly and half angrily. "Just one little spell, just a tiny one."

"Ah well," I sighed. "Just one, but only a little one."

I picked a book from the shelves and turned the pages.

"Yes, this'll do fine."

I pointed at myself, clicked my fingers twice, and the Prince's eyes nearly popped out of his head. Suddenly there was not one but *three* Witch Ways standing in front of him.

I clicked my fingers again and the others disappeared.

"How was that?" I smiled, pleased with myself.

"It was OK," he said, shrugging his shoulders.

"But I'd have preferred something better, like making a monster or a dragon or... "

"Little Prince, little Prince," I laughed. "There are two whole days for me to do things like that, and there are lots of good spells in these books." I ran my fingers across the books.

"Like this one for party spells, that one for curing spells, this one for monster spells and that one for... well, let me just say there are more spells than we ever need, but first you have to finish your breakfast and I have work to do – starting with your bedroom."

"You'll remember what you said, about not turning a fellow into a frog just because he made a bit of a mess, won't you?" he smiled nervously.

"Certainly I will," I chuckled, "and anyway, I'm sure I've seen far worse messes than anything you could have made."

But I hadn't.

The messiest room I'd ever seen was Hazel's. It was always so full of sweet wrappings, books, magazines and sweaty socks that sometimes you couldn't even see the floor, and there was so much dirt on her windows that little trees were growing on the glass. But never, never, ever had I seen anything like the Prince's room. It made Hazel's look like a palace.

My beautiful room!

I'd spent three days getting it to look beautiful and now, it looked like a rubbish tip that had been hit by a hurricane.

There was food splattered over the walls, the ceiling, the door, the floor and the windows. The curtains had been torn from the rails and rolled into a ball in the corner. The bed covers and pillows were torn to shreds, the legs of the bed were standing in four different corners of the room, and the wardrobe... Well, let's just say that I wouldn't have to chop firewood for some time.

I felt like crying. I knew the books said he might be upset, but I didn't think he'd be that upset. For a second, just for a very brief second, mind you, I felt the strongest urge to grab him by the neck and dangle him from the chimney. Then I started to feel guilty for thinking like that. It wasn't his fault. He was just very upset!

I looked from the mess, to the Prince and back again. He certainly looked happy now, and the mess wasn't anything that a quick tidying spell couldn't put right. So, I pointed at the room, said a few magic words and hey presto! It was as good as new again.

"Well, that's all the bad part over, and now we can settle down and start having fun with the Prince." I smiled at Tiddles, but he just groaned. If I'd have known what was coming I'd have groaned too.

Chapter 5

I know when you hear what happened next you'll say to yourself,

"Well, she was a bit silly, wasn't she!"

And you're right!

But you have to remember I didn't know what he was like. I thought he was just an ordinary little boy. So, when he started talking to me, and telling me all over again just how wonderful I was to be able to do such magic, I just said what I'd say if I was talking to you or your friends.

I pointed at my spell books, smiled and said, "But, it's not really me, little Prince. It's the books. All the magic is in the books. Anyone could do what I do. If they looked in the right books."

Tiddles pulled his paws over his eyes and groaned the strangest groan I had ever heard.

"Really?" said the Yuckee Prince, looking at the bookshelves.

"All the magic's in there, really?"

I just nodded and opened the door to the garden.

"Now, why don't you come and help me in the garden?"

He looked at the bookcase and then back at me.

"Er... if you don't mind, I'll stay here and rest for a moment or two."

"Well, I was rather looking forward to teaching you all about the garden," I said.

He sighed and took another quick glance at the books.

"Tell me," he said seriously, "have you ever turned a fellow into a frog or anything nasty?"

"Well once," I laughed, not bothering to add that it had been an accident in spell class and that it had taken days for Hazel to forgive me. "But I'll tell you all about it outside."

"Okay," he grumbled, "if you say so." And he pushed himself out of the chair and followed me into the garden.

Now, you probably know that we witches have a lot of spells that use animals and plants, and I don't mean all that "Eye of a newt, toe of a frog" rubbish you read about in fairy stories or see in pantos. I mean the real thing, like using the hair of a rabbit to get rid of cramp, or the feather of a dove to get rid of warts, or snake venom for curing coughs and lots of things like that.

Well, with all the animals and plants we need for potions and lotions we have quite a lot of work to do. So, for the next few hours the Yuckee Prince worked very hard, helping with all my jobs in the garden. And I'll tell you something, for someone who was not used to gardening or minding animals, he wasn't that bad. He made a few mistakes of course, but they were the sort anyone could make. At least I thought they were.

I mean, he didn't know that feeding the pigs hard nettles and thorns would have them running around in pain, trampling on all the plants, did he?

And when I said, "Feed the mice and the snakes," well, anyone could think I said, "Feed the mice to the snakes." Couldn't they?

(We did get them all back again, by the way.)

And you'll have to admit that, "Take the old mat and sling it on the rail," does actually sound a bit like, "Take the old cat and swing it by the tail." Doesn't it?

No. There was no doubt about it, he did seem to be working hard, but there was just one thing that I found annoying. He wouldn't stop asking me about the spells I could work.

Could I turn a boy into a pig?

Could I make horns grow on someone's head?

Could I make scabs and sores appear on someone's face?

Could I make someone as small as an ant?

Could I make someone float away like a loose balloon?

Could I make beasts and giants appear?

On and on and on and on he went.

And all I could say was, "Well, I know there's a spell somewhere in the book for that."

or

"Well, I'd have to look it up."

or

"Well, I know I have that written down somewhere."

Eventually, he just went very quiet for a while and I could see he was thinking of something. (What a pity I didn't know just what.)

"So you couldn't really do anything bad to a chap unless you had your books, could you?" he said at last.

"Well, not at the moment, little Prince," I replied honestly, thinking nothing of it. "I can make flowers grow big or small, and I can do a few food spells and tidying spells, and you've seen the one where I can make copies of myself appear but as for the others... I'd be lost without my books."

"I see," he yawned, giving me a rather strange look.

A few minutes later he stopped working and wiped his hands.

"It must be long past lunchtime" he smiled. "I'll go and make us something nice to eat."

"But wouldn't you like to help me clean out the other pig pen?"

"Oh... I don't think I could take any more excitement just yet." He smiled and skipped into the house, humming to himself.

"Well," I thought to myself. "I'm certainly glad that I read those books about babysitting. Everything is going just the way I thought it would. There's nothing that can go wrong now."

Oh, wasn't there?

Chapter 6

"Bang!" "Crash!" "Thump!" "Thud!"

It sounded like a war had started in the kitchen.

I raced into the cottage, expecting to find him lying horribly mangled under the bookcases or the cupboards.

And there he was... standing on the table clutching a large spell book muttering the magic words and making bottles of fizzy pop appear and splatter against the walls.

I looked at the bookcase. My precious books were scattered all over the floor.

"Little Prince! Stop it at once," I said crossly. "Stop, right now. This moment."

"Oh, shut up bird-brain. Why should you have all the fun?"

He pointed and mumbled, and a bottle of fizzy pop exploded right above my head.

"Little Prince, if you don't stop I'll... "

"You'll what?" he laughed horribly, making a bowl of custard topple all over my head. "You don't know how to do anything without your books, and I won't let you get them, so!

He pointed, said the magic words and a tub of treacle emptied all over us.

"Now this is what I call fun, not your stupid garden and animals."

I grabbed Tiddles and leapt back into the garden, pulling the door behind me as bottles and bowls of everything crashed all over the walls.

I knew that this was another of those tantrums I'd been reading about, and he was only doing it because he was sad, but it was such a bad one that I couldn't just ignore it and let him destroy my cottage. I had to do something, but what?

"Use your magic," I hear you say. "Use your magic on the little horror."

But I couldn't, not without my books, and he wasn't going to let me get to them, was he?

"What can I do? What can I do?" I moaned as I ran around the garden. "What can I do?"

The sound of smashing and breaking seemed to go on all day, though it probably only lasted about twenty-five or thirty minutes really. Then it stopped.

I started to crawl forward towards the cottage. Suddenly the window was thrown open and the Yuckee

Prince glared across at me. He was holding another spell book in his hand.

"Hey, fish-face, if you thought that was good wait till you see what I can do with this one. See that flea-bitten cat of yours?"

He pointed at Tiddles, and muttered a few words. The cat let out a terrified moan. Then, pop! A very large, very green and very frightened frog stood where Tiddles should have been.

"And if you think that's good, what about this?"

He began pointing and mumbling and laughing. Suddenly the whole garden was alive with flying rabbits, six-legged snakes, barking doves, and pigs as big as elephants.

"Stop it," I yelled. "Stop it at once. You're being naughty, very, very naughty."

"Stop? I'm only just starting. Wait till you see what I have planned for you." He ducked back into the cottage.

"Oh, what am I to do, what am I to do?"

As the Prince appeared back in the window, Tiddles hopped onto my broom and croaked loudly.

"What are you trying to tell me?" I said frantically. "What are you...?"

It was like a light going on in a dark room. I knew exactly what he was saying, and just in the nick of time too.

The Yuckee Prince leaned forward until he was almost hanging out of the window.

"Now, just wait and see what I've got for you."

"No, little prince. It's your turn for a surprise."

I pointed at my broom and muttered the magic words. It took off so fast that he didn't even see it. It flew over his shoulder, into the kitchen, turned and... just as it was about to lift him by the collar and carry him out to me, he ducked. It flew over his head and came straight at me. I jumped back in fright, tripped over Tiddles and landed flat on my back as the broom banged off the garden wall, bent into a boomerang shape and went spinning off towards the woods.

I rolled over onto my tummy and Tiddles hopped up beside my face, croaking and looking terrified.

"You rat bag," screamed the Yuckee Prince, as I tried to push myself up. "You horrid, ugly, rat bag. I was only going to turn you into a bunny or something, but you've tried to bash me with that broom. So try this."

He pointed at me and mumbled some words I'd never heard before.

Immediately, my nose started to itch and twitch. My fingers started to curl up and get smaller. My ears began to twitch and twist, and stretch so tight I felt as though they were going to pop off. Something started swishing across the back of my legs, and my whole body – arms, legs, face and everything – began to tingle and sting.

"Look here, you horror," I screamed, but I couldn't hear a word. All I could hear was a soft "squeak, squeak,

squeak," or something that sounded like that.

"Now for the next part," he screamed.

I heard him mumbling again.

Suddenly the frog was gone and there was a giant Tiddles looking down at me, with big frightened eyes. He'd turned Tiddles into a giant cat!

"Quick boy, go and get him! Get him!" I yelled.

But again all I could hear was that strange, "squeak, squeak squeak."

Tiddles looked at me and licked his lips. I knew that look. It meant "Food".

Oh, no! Tiddles was going to eat me.

"Run," I screamed to myself. "Get up and run."

But I couldn't get up. My body wouldn't work the way it should. I looked at my hands and screamed (or, at least, squeaked aloud). I didn't have any hands just tiny furry feet with little claws. I didn't have real feet either, just the same tiny furry things, with a tail swinging wildly between them. Then my nose started twitching. Oh no, there were whiskers in my nose. "I'm a mouse," I squeaked in terror. "A mouse. He hasn't turned Tiddles into a giant. He's turned me into a tiny mouse."

Tiddles had just decided the same thing. His eyes were still dull with confusion but he knew food when he saw it, and he started licking his lips even faster.

"Run, girl, run," I squeaked to myself.

Before I knew it I was scurrying across the garden, puffing and panting, and praying I could get to some hiding place before Tiddles ate me.

"Go on, puss, get her!" the Yuckee Prince roared with laughter. "Go on. Get her and gobble her up."

Poor old Tiddles, or maybe I should say good old Tiddles, was so confused by all the changing that had been going on that he didn't move. He just stood there licking his lips.

"Go on, you stupid moggy," screamed the Yuckee Prince, nearly falling out of the window. "Get her and gobble her up."

Tiddles might have been too confused to move, but not me. I raced across the garden, up the side of the rabbit hutch, and hid behind a box of carrots on the roof. Don't ask me how I managed to run up the side of the hutch because I've absolutely no idea, but I did it.

"Stupid puss. You've let her get away now," shouted the Yuckee Prince. "You stupid thing. Maybe you're too frightened of her. Maybe you should be a mouse, too."

He pointed at Tiddles, mumbled the words and suddenly there was another little mouse scurrying across the garden and up the shed.

"Oh, stay there," he snorted. "I'm having more fun. I'll deal with you later. So, stay there."

He needn't have bothered with that piece of advice. I hadn't the slightest intention of moving.

Chapter 7

Everywhere else in the kingdom the night was dark and peaceful but in my garden it was like a scene from your worst nightmare.

Hideous glowing monsters were rushing everywhere. Fire-breathing dragons with elephants' tusks were swooping down trying to carry off my pigs. Giant green worms with legs and mouths were trying to gobble up my hens. The goats were rushing around

the garden trying to avoid bears with bulls' heads and human arms, while something with a unicorn's horn, a tiger's head and a gorilla's body was swinging my snakes by their tails.

There was glowing slime flowing over the roof and into the flower beds; a snowstorm blowing in one part of the kitchen and the worst stink you can imagine coming from some weird plant that was growing through my chimney.

But the worst sight of all was the Prince, or rather the Princes, because sometime in the afternoon he must have found that spell I'd shown him earlier (remember the one where I made two copies of myself?) and now there were three of him. One was bad enough, so you can imagine how happy I was to see three.

I looked on helplessly as the three Yuckee Princes raced around the cottage and garden, screaming with laughter, pouring buckets of slush and slime over each other, and smashing and breaking anything that got in their way.

I was only glad they hadn't decided to go into the town. I dread to think what they could have done there.

"The Dame will kill me," I groaned as I watched the chaos below me. "The Dame will kill me. I have to think of something to stop this. Something, anything, oh, someone please come to my rescue. Help me end all this."

And someone did, even though they didn't mean to.

"I'm bored," moaned one of the Princes. "Really bored. We've magicked up all the food we can eat. We've made swimming pools and caves in the cottage. We've wrecked the garden, created monsters... there must be something we can do to have fun. Something really horrid and wicked."

"What about a great horrid giant?" said one.

"Yeah, a great horrid giant with a club," laughed another. "And we'll send him into town to smash and bash all those stinky people who are always so horrid to me."

The three of them clapped their hands and ran around the garden shouting with horrid delight.

"Huh, shows what they know," I said to myself, desperately trying to think of something I could do to stop them. " Giants are gentle and soft-hearted, not like the ones in fairytales. They're not giants at all they're..."

And my heart almost stopped beating. The Yuckee Prince was standing in the middle of the garden calling out a spell, but he wasn't calling up a giant. He was calling up an ogre, and real ogres are far worse than the ones in the stories.

He finished the spell and clicked his fingers. There was a loud roar and suddenly a terrible creature with one eye, sharp fangs and a twisted mouth was towering over the garden. He had a club in one hand, an axe in the other and a long sharp sword stuck in his belt.

He slowly looked around him at the Princes and the strange creatures, and began to drool.

"Hey, you!" shouted the Yuckee Prince. "I'm your master and I want you to... "

The Ogre looked down at him and gave a twisted smile.

"Little man boys," he slobbered. "Little man boys. Me like little man boys."

"Now listen here, you big oaf," shouted the Yuckee Prince. "I said I'm your master and I want... "

The Ogre didn't listen to him. He just looked around the garden muttering.

"Little man boys. Like little man boys, and strange creashures like them, too. Me like little man boys and strange creashures."

He put his axe down, swung his great three fingered hand and snatched up the giant worms and the bear things. He opened his mouth, threw them in and swallowed them all at one go.

"Creashures nice. Like creashures and little man boys. "

He swung his hand again, catching the dragons and the thing with the unicorn's horn and guzzled them in exactly the same way.

"Me like creashures. They nice. Like little man boys, too. Man boys taste nice." He looked at the Yuckee Princes.

The Princes began screaming and pushing each other out of the way as they dashed for the cottage. He scooped them up in his hand and looked at them.

"No, don't! Put us down," they cried. "Please put us down. Don't eat us."

The Ogre licked his lips and drooled all over his pimply chin.

"Like little man boys," he mumbled. "Nice. Taste good."

Then he slipped them into his pocket.

"Man boys nice. Not here. Find woods. Toast them."

He lumbered out of the garden towards the hills, and in three giant (or is it ogre?) steps he was out of sight.

"Serves the Yuckee Prince right," you say. "Let the Ogre eat him. He wasn't nice to anyone."

Well, that's not very nice of you.

I know he was bad, but I don't think anyone is bad enough to deserve that, although the Yuckee Prince came close. Anyway, if he did get eaten what would Dame Grimwood have said. I don't think it would have been, "Oh good job, Witch Way. Good job. I know there was a minor problem and he got eaten by an ogre he conjured up from your spell book while you were turned into a mouse and hiding on the roof of a rabbit hutch, but apart from that you did a really fine job."

No!

I don't think that would have been it.

I'd just have to save him.

But first I had to find some way of getting off the rabbit hutch without killing myself. Now if I'd

59

been a real mouse I'd have been off the roof and scampering down the side before you could say, "Smelly, stinky cheese!" but I wasn't a real mouse, was I?

I might have looked like a real mouse, squeaked like a real mouse, even twitched my nose like a real mouse but I still thought like a young witch, and even the thought of trying to climb down from something that high made my knees start knocking. Sorry! What's that you're saying? A rabbit hutch isn't very high?

Well maybe not to you but it is to a mouse. A mouse standing on a rabbit hutch would be about as far away from the ground as you would be if you were standing on five houses placed one on top of another. Would you like to try running down something that big?

No, I didn't thing so! And neither did I.

"Oh, how am I going to get down?" I moaned as I ran around the middle of the roof. "How am I ever going to get down?"

I soon found out.

Chapter 8

Tiddles noticed it before I did. He started running around the roof, squeaking and staring towards the wood in terror. I turned around and couldn't believe what I was seeing. It was the broomstick, bent like a boomerang and doing what a boomerang always does, spinning back to the place it was thrown from.

It came spinning over the garden wall, crashed into the rabbit hutch, and before you could say, "Yuckee Prince " the whole thing came crashing down, bringing Tiddles and I along with it.

I bounced off a rabbit, skidded into a clump of

hay and rolled over into the flower-beds.

"Well, that solves that problem," I said when I realised I didn't have anything broken or cut.

I scurried across the grass, up the step and into the cottage.

What a mess!

There was slime, goo, sticky stuff, water, bits of food, rags and broken furniture everywhere. And just in front of the Yuckee Prince's bedroom, there was a swamp with two crocodiles slowly paddling along. My books were all over the floor, but thankfully none of them seemed to be torn.

As the crocodiles looked at me through lazy eyes. I went scurrying across the floor hunting for the correct book. I found it stuck in a pile of snow near the front door. I nudged it open with my nose, and quickly, well not that quickly really, turned the pages by grabbing the corners with my teeth and running to the edge of the page.

When I found the page I was looking for I squeaked the changing spell and hey presto! I was back to myself.

I lifted the book, pointed at Tiddles and repeated the words, and he went rushing around the room mioawing with delight to be back to his old self.

I took another look at the room. It looked even worse now that I could see it properly. Still, I didn't have time to do anything now. I grabbed a book, called to Tiddles and raced into the yard.

"Quick Tiddles, onto the broomstick!" I yelled.

Then I stopped.

How could I ride a boomerang?

"Oh, no," I moaned. "I don't have time to go hunting for a spell to straighten this out. I'll just have to do the best I can."

I put my foot on one end, grabbed the other with my hands, and started pulling and tugging with every bit of strength I had.

I looked at the broomstick. It was still bending up

up to the right, but it was close enough.

As I said the magic words it began to hover. I put Tiddles on the back and hopped on. I tucked the book under my arm and clutched the neck of the broomstick with both hands, pointing it straight ahead towards the woods.

"Fly, Beauty," I commanded (well, what do you expect me to call my broomstick, Horace?) and she zoomed off, too high and too far to the left.

"Down," I snapped and we drifted down.

I jumped off, placed the neck of the broomstick over my knee and began pushing for all I was worth. I held it up and looked at it. It looked straight (well, straight-ish) now. It certainly wasn't pointing up any more.

I jumped back on, gave the command, and WOOSH! We were flying to the right, back towards my cottage.

"No!" I screamed in panic.

I couldn't waste anymore time stopping and starting. I didn't know where the Ogre was or, even worse, what he was doing, and I could only pray he hadn't eaten the Yuckee Prince yet.

I grabbed at the neck of the broomstick and jerked it back towards the woods, and for the next few minutes I had the most terrifying time – zooming above the clouds, wobbling this way and that as I fought with my broomstick trying to make it go in one direction while it struggled to go another.

Oh! It was such fun – I don't think! It was like riding a wild horse but in mid-air!

We finally managed to wobble our way across the treetops and... there was the Ogre. He was standing in a little clearing looking at a roaring fire.

"Hover," I whispered, and we stopped just far enough away so that he couldn't see us.

He fumbled in his pocket, pulled out one of the Yuckee Princes and dangled him in front of the fire.

"Boy man taste good," he drooled. "Taste much nice."
Pop!

The Yuckee Prince he was holding popped like a balloon and disappeared.

"Where he go? What happen?" the Ogre said dimly, as he jumped back in surprise.

"Where man boy go?"

I smiled with relief. Ogres are so stupid!

Everyone knows that if you spell up boys or girls or animals, they aren't real. They might look real, sound real and feel real, but they're no more real than one of those fancy balloons you can buy. (You know, the ones that look like people or animals.) And just like those balloons, if they get too hot they go "pop" and disappear.

"Get another one. Another boy man," groaned the Ogre, poking his hand in his pocket.

The one he pulled out this time was squealing and kicking and trying to bite his hand. (Which must have been a bit like trying to bite a mountain.)

"This one nice and lively. This boy man taste

nice."

He dangled him in front of the fire.

Pop!

Another Yuckee Prince disappeared.

"Where this one go?" yelled the Ogre angrily.

"Where this one go?"

He snatched out the real Yuckee Prince.

"Eat this one now, not let him go pop and go away. Eat him now." he said. "Now."

"No! Put me down," screamed the Yuckee Prince. "I know where there's a nice tasty witch, and a cat... and my mum and dad will be back soon... they'll be plump and tasty and there's the butcher and he's... "

But, fortunately, the Ogre didn't listen to him. He held the Yuckee Prince up to his mouth and drooled.

I was just about to fly down to him when he stopped and shook his head.

"No. Boy man's nice toasted. Like boy mans toasted," and he dangled the Yuckee Prince over the fire.

Now, I have to be honest and say that I'd set out without the slightest idea of how I was going to save the Yuckee Prince, and as I watched the Ogre dangling him over the fire I still didn't have a plan.

I thought about making the Ogre disappear, but if I did that the Yuckee Prince would just fall into the fire. I thought about shrinking the Ogre, but his Royal

Yuckeeness would still end up in the fire.

As I watched him dangling closer to the fire I knew I had to do something. Then, I had it!

Where I got the idea I don't know, but it was a good one.

I held onto the broom with one hand and tilted it slightly so that we'd be flying just below the Ogre's hand. I clutched the spell book with my free hand, and whispered,

"Fly."

I swooped down at the Ogre screaming as loud as I could. He looked up in surprise and I hurled the book as hard as I could, straight at his face. He jumped back and raised his hands to cover his eyes. As he did, the prince slipped between his fingers. I reached out, grabbed the Yuckee Prince by the hair, jerked him up onto the broomstick behind me and hurtled out of the forest.

As I looked back, I could see the Ogre angrily hurling my book onto the fire.

Oh, dear!

So much for the second part of my idea, which was to fly back, grab the book off the ground and cast a spell that would send the Ogre back to wherever it was he came from.

I pulled hard turning the broom towards the cottage. The Yuckee Prince was clinging tightly onto my shoulders and crying.

"Oh, thank you, thank you, thank you. You're so brave."

He was shaking with fear and this time I thought he actually meant what he said.

We came flying into my garden, and I ordered Beauty down.

The Yuckee Prince jumped down and threw his arms around my neck.

"Oh, thank you, thank you, thank you," he sobbed again. "Thank you for saving me. I am safe again."

THUD! THUD! THUD!

–came the rumbling from behind me. I spun around and shrieked with fear.

The Ogre was coming.

Chapter 9

If there were medals for being the fastest person to run from a garden into a cottage, we'd have all won gold. We were out of the garden and into the house before you could say "Ogre".

"There has to be a spell in one of these," I cried, frantically running around and looking at all of my books. "There has to be. Oh, if they were only in the right places I'd know which one was which."

"It's all my fault," sniffled the Yuckee Prince. "He's going to gobble us up and it's all because I was horrid."

"Oh, shut up and look through the books," I screamed at him sharply.

Whether it was because he was frightened, or whether it was because I sounded angrier than I have ever sounded in my life, I don't know, but the

Yuckee Prince looked shocked and then just said politely

"Certainly, Witch Way. I'm sorry."

I looked out of the window. The Ogre was about three steps away from the garden. What a good job they walk so slowly!

I was flicking through books and throwing them over my shoulder as fast as a budgie can fly. The Yuckee Prince was doing the same.

THUD!

The Ogre was two steps away and I didn't have the right spell.

THUD !

He was at the back wall, and still I didn't have a spell.

Oh! Why wasn't he a flower or a weed? Then I could shrink him with one of the spells I knew.

THUD!

He was in the back garden and lifting his club to smash the house. I put my hands over my face in fear. There was a crash, the sound of breaking glass and the Yuckee Prince was screaming, but it wasn't just a scream, it was words. There was a strange cracking sound then a funny swishing noise, but the house hadn't come down.

I opened one eye and peeked. The Yuckee Prince was hanging out of the window shaking with fear. He had a book in his hand, and the moon was shining through the branches of the great oak tree in the garden onto–

Oak tree! What oak tree? I didn't have an oak tree in my garden.

He couldn't have!

I walked out into the garden and looked at the tree. It towered above the cottage, and one large branch was raised as if it was just about to come crashing through the roof.

He'd done it!

The Yuckee Prince had turned the Ogre into a giant oak.

"I suppose I should thank you," I said angrily to him.

"Not really," he sniffed, looking at the ground. "It was all my fault. I'm sorry."

I heard him, but I didn't believe him. I'd had enough of his Royal Yuckeeness, and I didn't care what the books said about him being naughty because he was sad. I'd decided he was just naughty because he liked being naughty.

Oh, sure he was sorry now – who wouldn't be if they'd just nearly been eaten or flattened by an ogre – but tomorrow. Well, that would be another day.

I looked around the garden, and the house. What a mess.

"Can I help you tidy up?" he asked.

"No," I snapped "You've done quite enough. Just go to your room and stay there. Oh, and mind you don't fall into the crocodile swamp."

He just put his head down and shuffled off to his bedroom, carefully avoiding the crocodiles.

What's that you say? I was being very mean to him?

Well, if you don't mind me saying so, that sounds nice coming from someone who thought I should let the Ogre eat him, doesn't it ?

But you're right, I was being mean to him, and as you know that's not really like me at all. The thing was, now that it was all over I suddenly realised just how much worse it could have been, and I was feeling rather frightened at the thought of it.

I could have been eaten by Tiddles.

I could have been crushed by the Ogre.

Even worse, the Yuckee Prince could have been eaten and left me to face Dame Grimwood!

Or what if he'd have found a worse spell and turned me into a tree or... or... or...

It was so frightening that I just didn't want to think about it, and I was just a little bit annoyed at the Yuckee Prince.

Do you blame me?

I walked into the cottage. The place was a mess, and I knew it would take more than a simple tidying spell to put it all back in order, and I was right.

I don't know how long it took, but I do know that by the time I'd put the last book on the shelf the sun had been out for a long, long time.

The cottage was back in order. The damage he'd done to my animals had been undone. Well, the snakes were exhausted from running around like greyhounds, and the doves' throats were really sore from barking like dogs all day, but at least they were a bit more normal.

I was so exhausted that all I wanted to do was fall asleep.

The rest of the tidying could wait until later.

I opened the door to the Yuckee Prince's room.

He was fast asleep. Funny how sweet he looked when he was asleep.

As I closed his bedroom door I looked across at my books. I knew that I'd only sleep for a little while and that I'd be up long before him, but even so I decided it might be a good idea to put a special spell on my books so that he couldn't go near them – just in case.

When I reached my bedroom I was so tired I almost crawled into bed.

"Just a little sleep," I said closing my eyes. "Just a catnap."

Chapter 10

Some catnap!

I'd probably still be asleep if it wasn't for the singing somewhere in the distance.

I yawned, pushed myself out of bed and looked out of the window.

"What? It couldn't be!"

My eyes nearly popped out of my head. The royal carriage was just coming over the hill and behind it the sun was going down slowly.

"Now just a minute," you say. "Don't you mean the sun was just coming up?"

No, I don't. I mean going down.

I'd been so tired that I'd slept right through the day and into the night.

Suddenly my heart started pounding.

If I'd slept all day that meant the Yuckee Prince had been on his own, and if he'd been on his own all day he could have...

"AAAARRRGH!"

I raced to the mirror. My hair was still on my head, it wasn't painted green. I didn't have spots or stripes all over my face. So, at least he hadn't done anything to me.

But there were still lots and lots of other things he could have done to "amuse" himself, such as smashing my plates, chopping up my furniture, tearing my curtains, or frightening my animals and I bet he'd done them all.

"Oh, how could I have been so stupid?" I moaned, as I broke the world record for getting dressed. "How could I be so one hundred per cent stupid, how could I?"

I pulled the door open, rushed into the kitchen and...

The Yuckee Prince was sitting by the fire staring at the flames. Tiddles was stretched out at his feet, chewing on the remains of a giant sausage, and everything looked absolutely, perfectly normal.

There wasn't a thing out of place. There wasn't anything smashed or torn. There wasn't a pile of rubbish in the middle of the floor. There weren't any frightened animals running around.

What was he up to?

I glanced at the table.

There was a large bowl of steaming porridge, a plate of fruit, a glass of nettle tea, and a large bunch of fresh flowers in a jar all set out neatly on a silver tray.

What was he up to?

"I made you something to eat," he said softly. "I hope you like it."

I walked over to the chair, picked it up and shook it hard but nothing happened. There weren't any pins on it, the legs didn't fall off and the back didn't come away in my hand.

"It must be the food," I said to myself as I sat down slowly.

"That's it. He's done something to the food."

I dipped a spoon into the porridge, stirred it around, lifted a spoonful and tipped it back into the bowl.

Nothing!

No dead mice, no worms, no broken glass, no rusty nails.

Nothing.

I did it three more times just to be sure.

"I haven't done anything wrong," he said, sniffling and biting his lips. "All I did was do a bit of dusting, feed Tiddles and make your meal. I wish you could believe me. I really do."

I took a tiny taste of the porridge. It was fine. No, it was better than fine. It was the creamiest, softest porridge I'd ever tasted.

Maybe he hadn't done anything after all.

No! He must have!

I took a sip of the nettle tea. It was wonderful.

Just the way I liked it. He'd even added the extra honey and mustard.

I couldn't believe it.

He really hadn't done anything to it.

"Is everything okay?" he sniffled "is ev...?"

Suddenly he let out a loud cry and started sobbing and wiping his nose with his sleeve.

"It's not fair!" he sobbed. "It's not fair at all. I know I was mean and horrid yesterday b... b... b... but now I... I... I... I'm trying to be n... n... n... nice and you w... w... w... won't believe me. Y... y... y... you w... w... w...w..."

He placed his head on his arms and sobbed so hard that his whole body shook like a jelly.

Now, you can call me a big softie if you like but as I sat there watching him shaking and sobbing, all my anger and suspicion just melted away. I mean, I know he'd been really naughty before but he had been trying to make up for it. And before I knew what was happening I was feeling so sorry for him that there were tears running down my cheeks.

I jumped off the chair and ran over and put my arm around him.

"There, there, little Prince. Don't cry. Please, don't cry. "

I patted him softly on the head. "Please don't cry."

"I'm s... s... s... s... sorry I... I... I... I... was s... s... so naughty," he sobbed. "I... I... I... I really am but I w... w... won't do it a... g... g... gain. I... I promise. I... I... w... w... as so frightened. The g... g... giant and all that. I won't d... d... d... do it again, honest. I p... p... p... p... promise."

So that was it!

He hadn't been up to anything at all.

The Ogre had frightened the living daylights out of him.

Well, I've always said there's nothing like nearly getting toasted, roasted, eaten or trampled by an ogre to make a chap change his ways, and it had certainly made the little Prince change his.

"And long may it last," I smiled to myself. "Long may it last."

"Oh, well let's forget all about that, now." I said softly, rubbing his hair.

"But I was so frightened," he sniffed wiping his nose with the arm of his velvet jacket, and not just the Ogre. I was frightened that you would be so angry you'd want to turn me into something horrid."

"Me, little Prince?" I smiled gently. "I told you before, I'd never do a thing like that."

"Wouldn't you, really? "

"No. I promise. Witches honour. I'd never do that."

Now he was smiling again.

"Even though I caused so much trouble?"

"Of course not, little Prince."

Now don't ask me why I said what came next because I've absolutely no idea. Maybe it was because I wanted to cheer him up, or maybe it was a sudden attack of madness. I honestly don't know, but as the front gate opened and the King and Queen walking up the path I heard myself blurting out the words I was soon going to regret.

"Well it wasn't really your fault, was it? I should have been more careful with you. I should have known my spell books would be tempting for a little boy like you."

"Really?" sniffed the Prince. "No one would blame me for what happened?"

"Of course not little Prince."

"Then would they blame you?" he asked with a twinkle in his eye.

"I suppose so," I replied, starting to feel a little nervous.

"And you could get in trouble?"

"Well, er... I suppose I could."

Suddenly I was shaking with fear because there was no "could" about it. If anyone ever found out I'd be in real trouble, and I don't mean the "You bold child, go to your room" sort of trouble you could get into. I mean big trouble, *big, big, trouble.*

And I could only guess what the punishment would be. At best I'd probobly be thrown out of the kingdom and made to start school all over again and at worst... Oh Gosh! At worst I'd probobly be dragged off to the axe man or thrown into a dungeon forever and ever and ever.

Crumbs, I was in a real mess.

"You know, I hadn't thought about that," said the little Prince, jumping to his feet and skipping to the door. "I hadn't thought that you could get into trouble over everything. I really hadn't, not until you just mentioned it."

And to be honest I don't think he had.

Oh me and my big mouth!

Chapter 11

"Oh, Witch Way, Witch Way. We're here," called the King, tapping on the door. "We've come to collect our little hor... er, our little boy."

The Prince unbolted the front door and the King and Queen shuffled in, sadly.

"Well," sighed the King wearily, "and how has my little boy been enjoying himself for the last two days?"

As the little Prince turned around there was something in his smile that made me feel very, very uneasy.

"You see that Witch," he said pointing at me. "Do you know what she did? She let me get carried away... "

"... She let me get carried away by... " He repeated it slowly, and suddenly my heart started racing and my eyes opened wide with fear.

He was going to tell them!

He was going to tell them – everything!

I fell down onto my hands and knees ready to plead for mercy.

"She let me get carried away by... all the fun I was having in the garden."

What?

What was that?

Carried away by all the fun he was having in the garden?

All the fun I was having in the garden!

Did I hear him correctly or was fear scrambling my hearing?

All the fun I was having in the garden!

No ogre?

No toasting over fires?

No bad stuff?

Just – *All the fun I was having in the garden!*

I looked up at him, my tummy was rumbling with fear but he just smiled sweetly.

Phew!

He'd only been teasing me.

"Do come and see what we did in the garden," he smiled to the King and Queen. "Come and see."

"Are you all right, Witch Way," asked the King looking at me as I knelt on all fours.

"Yes it... it... er... it's er... j... j... j... just I... I... I... I... dropped s... s... something." I was still trying to recover from the Prince's little joke.

"It's an invisible... er... thingy Oh, h... h... h... here it is," I fibbed, pretending to pick something off the floor before I climbed to my feet.

He really had me going for a minute.

The Prince unbolted the back door and led the King and Queen by the hand out into the garden.

The last time I'd seen my garden it had been an absolute mess, but now – well, I could hardly believe my eyes. It looked beautiful. Absolutely beautiful. The rabbit hutch was standing again and freshly painted. All the fences and animal pens that had been scattered in pieces over the garden were back to the way they had been. The flowers and bushes had all been replanted. All the herbs had been re-labelled and divided into groups. The mud and the slime had been cleaned away, and there was even a new pebble path running around the border. He must have been working all day to get it looking this good.

"And you did all this with Witch Way?" the King asked in amazement.

"Yes, and do you know something. I really enjoyed it."

He looked at me and smiled, and there was a wicked glint in his eyes again.

I felt myself start to shudder.

"Let me tell you about this tree and me." He said, tapping the oak tree.

"This tree was once a giant... "

My legs began to tremble and there was sweat running down my neck.

"This tree was once a giant... "

"No, please, no! Don't!" I screamed inwardly. "Please don't. Don't tell them."

"A giant acorn!" he snapped, laughing as he watched me almost collapsing with fear.

"No, that's not right," he giggled. "It wasn't a giant. It was an ogre... an ogre... an ogre... "

This was too much!

I was shaking like a leaf and so full of fear that I felt I could get sick any minute.

"... an ogre... an ogregrown acorn. That's right." he giggled. "An ogregrown acorn."

I felt myself go weak and clutched at the King's sleeve.

"Why, poor Witch Way," said the King putting

his arm around my shoulders. "You've gone quite pale and you're absolutely trembling with the cold."

"Oh, I do hope it's nothing to do with me," giggled his Royal Yuckeeness, enjoying himself.

I was shaking so much that the King practically had to lift me into the cottage and help me into a chair. As he did so, I noticed that his face had turned almost white. I wasn't the only one who was worried.

The King stared at the ground and drew a little circle with his toe.

"About those... er, lollies we promised," he said, coughing nervously.

"We sort of forgot them. But don't worry. We'll buy you a new toy or ten to make up for it... honest... honest we will," he gabbled it all out in one quick breath. Then he closed his eyes waiting for the Prince to have another of those famous tantrums and start throwing things around the place.

"Oh, don't worry about the lollies," grinned the Yuckee one. " I don't need them or a new toy. I can think of only one thing I want to play with from now on."

He glanced quickly at my books and then back at me. He did it so quickly that no one else would have really noticed. But he wanted me to notice.

My poor heart was beating so fast that any minute now I expected it would just pop out of my chest and land at my feet.

He walked over, bent down and stroked Tiddles fur.

"This is all I want," he said softly.

"A cat," sighed the King, relieved. "You want another cat. Certainly, have five, ten or twenty."

"Oh, I don't want a new one," he said winking at me. "I want to be able to come back and play with Tiddles real soon, and I do hope Witch Way will let me."

He stopped and shot another and very quick glance at my spell books and then turned back to me and smiled as he whispered the words "Or else" so softly that only I could hear.

I couldn't move or speak.

I just sat there shaking.

"Well you certainly seem to have made a big impression here, Witch Way," said the Queen turning away to hide her tears.

"He's so much more gentle and loving. My, look at the sky, I think we should be getting home."

"I think so," said the Prince, taking her hand and leading her into the cottage. "At least for now."

"I must say, Witch Way," said the King, as he helped me out of the chair, "he does seem to be somewhat different to the little chap we dropped here."

Then he dropped his voice to a whisper, "You won't believe this, but he can be a bit of a handful at times!"

He put his arm around my shoulder and led me out of the front door and down the path to the front gate.

"Why you poor child, you are absolutely trembling. You could be coming down with something. Maybe I should leave the little Prince here to look after you for a while."

My knees buckled and I clung to the front gate to stop myself collapsing, but I still managed to shake my head.

"Oh, well. If you say so but I'm sure he wouldn't mind staying a little longer. He seems so happy. It's like magic. Pure magic. He really must come on another visit sometime."

"Yes, and real soon," smiled the Yuckee Prince with that twinkle in his eye. "Just think of all the fun we'll have then."

I gasped in terror but the King must have thought that it was a "whoop" of joy because suddenly he was shaking my hand firmly and saying, "Good, good, then that's settled. I'll try to arrange that soon."

"Real soon," added the Prince laughing. "Really, really soon."

I wanted to scream but my mouth just opened and closed without a word coming out. My voice had fled in fear.

"Oh, Aly," smiled her Royal Silliness. "Witch Way is so excited at the idea, she's quite overcome."

As the royal carriage pulled away, I raced back to my cottage and slammed the door behind me.

Another visit from the Yuckee Prince?

Suddenly my voice was shocked back into life and I heard myself saying the only thing that could show how I felt about that.

"AAAAARRRGGGGHHH!"

Watch out for some other great books from:
BLACKWATER PRESS

Following a walk on Slieve Gullion, a strange creature stalks John Kett. Curious things begin to happen. Rex the dog mews, the Ketts fly and Mary Kett almost gets 'to jump out of a nut'. Granny clashes with Olivia Jolson, the famous theatrical director, during the staging of the pageant to celebrate the finding of the 'Gretel Stones'.

Meanwhile... events draw them all towards the Mountains of the Hag, where they are eagerly awaited by... The Cally.

BLACKWATER PRESS

Ignatius Mac Taggle is no ordinary pig. Noble and refined, yet lovable too, he lives in the lap of luxury at Ballymactaggle Hall but then his world is turned upside down. His friends, Lucy and Gavin, lend their support as he sets about making his master's dream of helping old unwanted donkeys a reality. They have to contend, however, not only with the scheming Peregrine, the new owner at the Hall, but also with the tricks of Lucy's arch rival, Rachel.

Can Ignatius and Lucy outwit their enemies, or will Peregrine and Rachel have the last laugh, after all?